The Minutes

by Tracy Letts

ISBN 978-0-573-70718-6

www.concordtheatricals.com
www.concordtheatricals.co.uk

FOR PRODUCTION INQUIRIES

UNITED STATES AND CANADA
info@concordtheatricals.com
1-866-979-0447

UNITED KINGDOM AND EUROPE
licensing@concordtheatricals.co.uk
020-7054-7298

Each title is subject to availability from Concord Theatricals Corp., depending upon country of performance. Please be aware that THE MINUTES may not be licensed by Concord Theatricals Corp. in your territory. Professional and amateur producers should contact the nearest Concord Theatricals Corp. office or licensing partner to verify availability.

No one shall make any changes in this title(s) for the purpose of production. No part of this book may be reproduced, stored in a retrieval system, scanned, uploaded, or transmitted in any form, by any means, now known or yet to be invented, including mechanical, electronic, digital, photocopying, recording, videotaping, or otherwise, without the prior written permission of the publisher. No one shall share this title(s), or any part of this title(s), through any social media or file hosting websites.

For all inquiries regarding motion picture, television, online/digital and other media rights, please contact Concord Theatricals Corp.

MUSIC AND THIRD-PARTY MATERIALS USE NOTE

Licensees are solely responsible for obtaining formal written permission from copyright owners to use copyrighted music and/or other copyrighted third-party materials (e.g., artworks, logos) in the performance of this play and are strongly cautioned to do so. If no such permission is obtained by the licensee, then the licensee must use only original music and materials that the licensee owns and controls. Licensees are solely responsible and liable for clearances of all third-party copyrighted materials, including without limitation music, and shall indemnify the copyright owners of the play(s) and their licensing agent, Concord Theatricals Corp., against any costs, expenses, losses and liabilities arising from the use of such copyrighted third-party materials by licensees. For music, please contact the appropriate music licensing authority in your territory for the rights to any incidental music.

IMPORTANT BILLING AND CREDIT REQUIREMENTS

If you have obtained performance rights to this title, please refer to your licensing agreement for important billing and credit requirements.

The world premiere of *THE MINUTES* was produced and presented at Steppenwolf Theatre Company (Anna D. Shapiro, Artistic Direictor; David Schmitz, Executive Director) in Chicago, Illinois, on November 9, 2017. The performance was directed by Anna D. Shapiro, with scenic design by David Zinn, costume design by Ana Kuzmanic, lighting design by Brian MacDevitt, and sound design and original music by Andre Pluess. The stage manager was Christine D. Freeburg. The cast was as follows:

MR. PEEL	Cliff Chamberlain
MAYOR SUPERBA	William Petersen
MS. JOHNSON	Brittany Burch
MR. BLAKE	James Vincent Meredith
MR. BREEDING	Kevin Anderson
MR. HANRATTY	Danny McCarthy
MR. ASSALONE	Jeff Still
MS. INNES	Penny Slusher
MS. MATZ	Sally Murphy
MR. OLDFIELD	Francis Guinan
MR. CARP	Ian Barford

CHARACTERS

MR. PEEL
MAYOR SUPERBA
MS. JOHNSON
MR. BLAKE
MR. BREEDING
MR. HANRATTY
MR. ASSALONE
MS. INNES
MS. MATZ
MR. OLDFIELD
MR. CARP

Note: Innes and Oldfield should be older than the others.

SETTING

A city council meeting room

And I can see that something else died there in the bloody mud, and was buried in the blizzard. A people's dream died there. It was a beautiful dream.
– Black Elk

Kill and scalp all, big and little; nits make lice.
– Col. John Milton Chivington

(At rise:)

*(**PEEL**, wearing an overcoat and holding a briefcase, stands downstage. He is soaking wet.)*

*(Prior to rise, upstage, **JOHNSON** was showing **MAYOR SUPERBA** a document...but **PEEL**'s entrance has interrupted them.)*

(Sound of heavy rain.)

SUPERBA. Peel.

PEEL. Hello, Mr. Mayor.

SUPERBA. *(Crossing to **PEEL**.)* Good to have you back.

PEEL. Thank you.

SUPERBA. My condolences.

PEEL. Thank you.

SUPERBA. How old was your mother?

PEEL. Seventy-six.

SUPERBA. Young, these days. Father still alive?

PEEL. No.

SUPERBA. Mm. I've lost both of mine too. Tough spot. It's disorienting...for a while. You feel untethered. Well, I suppose you are. How were the services?

> *(**BLAKE** enters, removes his coat, lingers.)*

PEEL. Really, it's a blur.

SUPERBA. She wasn't from here, was she?

PEEL. No. The coast. My wife's from here. Her parents are getting older so we moved here a couple of years ago to be close to them.

SUPERBA. Right. Well. You seem like you're bearing up. Welcome back. Let me know if I can do anything.

PEEL. Thank you.

> (As **SUPERBA** moves away...)

How was last week? Did I miss anything?

SUPERBA. We're on track.

> (**SUPERBA** exits. **BLAKE** drifts out after him. During the following, **JOHNSON** passes out paperwork, rolls out a snack cart, etc.)

PEEL. I'm Peel.

JOHNSON. I know.

PEEL. Okay. It's just that I'm new and I missed last week. So I've only been to a couple of meetings. Two.

JOHNSON. I know.

PEEL. So I wasn't sure if you remembered me.

JOHNSON. I know who you are.

PEEL. I'm still learning the lay of the land.

JOHNSON. It takes a while.

PEEL. How long have you been the clerk?

JOHNSON. A few years.

PEEL. You have an awful lot of responsibility.

JOHNSON. I knew what I was signing up for.

PEEL. Still. It's a lot.

> (Pause.)

Man, it's really coming down out there.

(**JOHNSON** *smiles politely.*)

Do you like it?

(Quick beat.)

Being the clerk?

JOHNSON. It's needed.

PEEL. I understand *that*. I didn't. I didn't understand that until I had my first child. I never considered public service before then. But after my girl was born, I thought, well, I can sit around complaining about everything or I can pitch in and make Big Cherry a better place to live. *Try.*

(*He shows* **JOHNSON** *a photo on his iPhone.*)

JOHNSON. She's lovely.

PEEL. Justine. Eighteen months. Do you have children?

JOHNSON. Mm. A daughter.

PEEL. Great. How old?

JOHNSON. Five. Almost five.

PEEL. Great. What's her name?

JOHNSON. Evie.

PEEL. Nice. Do you have a picture?

JOHNSON. I don't think so.

PEEL. You, uh, I've met your husband, I think. He owns the steakhouse?

JOHNSON. That's right.

PEEL. I met him at the Kiwanis pancake supper.

JOHNSON. Mm.

PEEL. I joined the Kiwanis.

> *(Longer pause.)*

JOHNSON. *(A little forced.)* So you're a *joiner*.

PEEL. I guess I am. You know, moving to a new town and having a baby, it's just opened up a lot of things. And my wife is at home with Justine so I feel an obligation to be more social. So I joined the Kiwanis and we started playing bridge, my wife and I. And I ran for this seat.

JOHNSON. And you got elected.

PEEL. Yeah, I still can't believe that. My mom actually warned me not to do it.

JOHNSON. Why is that?

PEEL. She thought I'd be too eager to please. She said, "The first time you have to vote 'no' on someone else's idea, you're going to have a panic attack."

JOHNSON. Do you have panic attacks?

PEEL. No, no, she was exaggerating. She was funny.

JOHNSON. Sorry about your mother.

PEEL. Thank you.

> *(Lights in the room flicker, dim, then buzz back full.)*

Is that something that happens?

JOHNSON. The grid. It's really old.

PEEL. Who's Evie's dentist?

> *(**JOHNSON** looks at him.)*

Sorry. I'm a dentist. Pediatric dentist.

JOHNSON. We see Dr. Crain.

PEEL. Sure. Very good. Oh, hey, I wasn't trying... I wasn't *soliciting*.

JOHNSON. I know.

PEEL. Just professional curiosity.

JOHNSON. It's fine.

PEEL. Boy, old Crain really has it sewn up around here, doesn't he?

> *(Beat.)*

Did I miss anything, last week? I heard some of the fellows in the parking lot talking about Mr. Carp.

JOHNSON. I'm sure you'll learn what you need to know.

> *(**BLAKE** re-enters as **BREEDING, ASSALONE,** and **HANRATTY** drift into the room from outside. Coats, briefcases. **HANRATTY** carries large posters wrapped in a plastic sheet. **BREEDING** is in the middle of a story.)*

BREEDING. ....Jim Rutherford? Editor of the *Record*, big guy, used to play tight end for the Savages. Anyway, Sunday afternoon we're out at Iroquois, the eighteenth hole. Jim's a good golfer too, carries a seven handicap. He's forty yards from the cup, great lie, decides to punch it with a wedge, steps up...and he shanks it!

> *(He anticipates a laugh, doesn't get it.)*

HE SHANKS IT!

> *(He roars with laughter. The other **MEMBERS** laugh politely, go about their business. **MATZ** enters from outside.)*

BLAKE. Peel.

PEEL. Hello, Mr. Blake.

BLAKE. Surprised to see you here.

PEEL. Why is that?

BLAKE. I thought you'd take some time.

PEEL. I had ten days. That's enough.

BLAKE. Ten days wouldn't even begin to satisfy me. What I wouldn't give to pack it all up and head to the coast, forever. That's the life. Stone drunk in the direct rays of the sun, best way to pass through this world. Instead of living inside this wet sock of a town.

PEEL. Nobody's stopping you, Mr. Blake.

BLAKE. Are you making a joke?

PEEL. Not intentionally.

BLAKE. What did he want?

PEEL. Who?

BLAKE. Superba.

PEEL. Just condolences.

BLAKE. Ah. For who?

PEEL. For me. For my mother.

BLAKE. Right.

      (Pause.)

Sorry about your mother.

PEEL. Thank you. What happened last week?

BLAKE. What happened.

PEEL. The meeting, last week. Did something happen with Mr. Carp?

BLAKE. Who have you spoken to?

PEEL. What do you mean? No one.

BLAKE. You've spoken to no one.

PEEL. I'm speaking to you.

BLAKE. You've spoken to no one.

PEEL. I just got back.

BLAKE. But you said you heard about Carp.

PEEL. Just now, coming in, I overheard some talk about Mr. Carp.

BLAKE. Superba didn't mention Carp, did he?

PEEL. No. Should he have?

BLAKE. I'm not sure it's my responsibility.

PEEL. What isn't?

BLAKE. Catching you up.

PEEL. Not your responsibility.

BLAKE. Carp is no longer on the council.

PEEL. *What?*

BLAKE. He understood I couldn't speak on his behalf, on behalf of his *cause*. I have to see which way the wind is blowing.

PEEL. Which way is the wind blowing?

BLAKE. "An ill wind bloweth no man to good."

PEEL. The wind bloweth?

BLAKE. The wind bloweth all right.

(**HANRATTY** *approaches.*)

HANRATTY. Peel.

PEEL. Hello, Mr. Hanratty.

HANRATTY. Blake.

BLAKE. Hanratty.

HANRATTY. What about this rain?

BLAKE. What about it?

HANRATTY. It's raining.

BLAKE. Tell me about it.

HANRATTY. It's been raining for two weeks.

BLAKE. I live here.

HANRATTY. My condolences.

PEEL. Thank you.

HANRATTY. You feeling all right? Aside from the obvious.

PEEL. I feel fine.

HANRATTY. You look peaked. *("Peaked" pronounced with one syllable.)*

PEEL. I'm not sure you're saying that right.

HANRATTY. Ragged. *("Ragged" pronounced with one syllable.)*

PEEL. No, I feel well. Yourself?

HANRATTY. Better than usual actually. Flush with positive ions.

BLAKE. You *do* look well.

HANRATTY. Thank you.

BLAKE. Very healthy.

HANRATTY. Thank you.

BLAKE. You eat nuts.

HANRATTY. Sorry?

BLAKE. You must eat nuts. They're the reason you look oily. Well-oiled.

HANRATTY. Okay.

BLAKE. Nuts have a lot of essential oils.

HANRATTY. Yes, I eat nuts.

PEEL. Listen, what is the story with Mr. Carp?

BLAKE. Peel's only now learning about Carp.

HANRATTY. Shame about Carp.

PEEL. Is it?

HANRATTY. Yes. *I* think so. A man down.

PEEL. Down *how*?

BLAKE. A bad man down is no tragedy.

PEEL. Mr. Carp isn't a bad man.

BLAKE. I didn't say he was.

HANRATTY. And I didn't say it was a tragedy. I said it was a shame.

PEEL. I'd like to know what happened, exactly –

HANRATTY. Hey, Peel, the accessible fountain is on the docket tonight.

PEEL. I told you I'd support that.

HANRATTY. Right, but is it half-hearted support? Is your attitude casual? I'd like to know I can count on you. I know it's not your bill. But it's a cause you can believe in.

PEEL. Yes, I believe in it. I believe in inclusion.

HANRATTY. Inclusion, right, I think it's important that we reach out to everybody.

PEEL. Everybody.

HANRATTY. I mean, the unrepresented.

BLAKE. No one's representing them.

HANRATTY. I still think we need to reach out to them, even if we don't have any of them on our board.

BLAKE. Because his sister is handicapped.

HANRATTY. My God, Blake, are you behind on the nomenclature. "Handicapped" went out with sodomy laws.

BLAKE. Don't we still have sodomy laws?

HANRATTY. Hoop skirts.

(**INNES** *enters from outside.*)

BLAKE. I know, I know, the correct term is –

BLAKE.	**HANRATTY.**
"Impaired."	"Disabled."

BLAKE. "Impaired."

HANRATTY. "Disabled."

BLAKE. I don't think so, Harry.

HANRATTY. No, I'm certain about this. We reviewed the semantics.

BLAKE. Who's we? What kind of review?

HANRATTY. My guys. The accessible fountain men. We did a study.

PEEL. You have accessible fountain men?

HANRATTY. You can't get anything done on your own.

BLAKE. You did a study on the nomenclature?

HANRATTY. On the semantics.

BLAKE. What's the difference?

HANRATTY. Impairment is the source of disability.

BLAKE. No, what's the difference between semantics and nomenclature?

HANRATTY. They're different words. Look, Peel, I'm not asking you to wave a flag but any support you can give on behalf of the bill would be greatly appreciated. And your vote of course. Greatly appreciated.

PEEL. You have my support but I really want to get the story on Mr. Carp –

HANRATTY. What about you, Blake?

BLAKE. It all depends, doesn't it?

HANRATTY. Does it?

BLAKE. Would you consider my support a favor?

HANRATTY. Yes, it would be a favor. I would consider that a favor.

BLAKE. A favor to be repaid.

HANRATTY. Oh, I see, so you'll support my bill if I support Lincoln Smackdown.

BLAKE. If you vote for Lincoln Smackdown, I will blow my hooter in support of your handicap bill.

HANRATTY. Disabled.

BLAKE. Infirm.

HANRATTY. What?

BLAKE. Sorry. "Deformity."

HANRATTY. No.

BLAKE. Wasn't that it? No! Infirmity?

HANRATTY. Impairment.

BLAKE. Now that doesn't sound right.

HANRATTY. Lincoln Smackdown is a ludicrous idea.

BLAKE. That's what they said about Social Security.

HANRATTY. You can't compare Social Security to Lincoln Smackdown.

(**ASSALONE** *approaches.*)

ASSALONE. Peel.

PEEL. Hello, Mr. Assalone.

ASSALONE. Sorry about your mom.

PEEL. Thank you.

ASSALONE. How did she go?

PEEL. Stroke.

ASSALONE. That a gal.

(**ASSALONE** *moves off.*)

HANRATTY. Oh listen, Peel, since Carp's gone, I've lost a partner for squash. Someone told me you play.

PEEL. I've had to give it up. At least until I have surgery on my labrum.

BLAKE. Your what?

PEEL. My labrum.

BLAKE. You have a labrum?

PEEL. I tore my labrum and until I have the surgery, I can't play squash.

HANRATTY. Can I have your racket?

PEEL. What?

HANRATTY. If you're not playing, you won't need your racket.

PEEL. No.

HANRATTY. Can I have it?

PEEL. Why do you want it?

HANRATTY. Nice to have an extra. And if I play with someone else who doesn't have a racket.

PEEL. Yes, but once I've recovered from my surgery –

HANRATTY. Of course. When are you having the surgery?

PEEL. I haven't decided. Maybe this winter.

HANRATTY. You could die before then. And then your racket would just get chucked out with all the other stuff. This way's better. Bring it in next week.

*(**BREEDING** approaches. **HANRATTY** moves off.)*

BREEDING. Peel.

PEEL. Mr. Breeding.

BREEDING. Good to see you again. Sorry about your mother.

*(**OLDFIELD** enters from outside.)*

PEEL. Thank you.

BREEDING. Were the two of you close?

PEEL. Very.

BREEDING. That's tough then. I hated my mother. Still do. And she's lost her mind. Tape?

*(**BREEDING** offers **PEEL** a breath strip.)*

PEEL. No, thank you. Looks like I missed an important meeting last week.

BREEDING. What's *important*? A hundred years from now, will anyone care?

PEEL. Well, if you look at it like that, why show up at all?

BREEDING. Exactly. Good to have you back. We need more of your kind around here.

*(**BREEDING** moves off.)*

PEEL. Blake!

BLAKE. What?

PEEL. What in the world happened with Mr. Carp?!

*(**SUPERBA** re-enters.)*

BLAKE. Piece of advice: stay agile. "In politics, entrenchment is synonymous with folly."

PEEL. Who said that?

BLAKE. I don't know, Hobbes, maybe.

SUPERBA. I think we have a quorum.

BLAKE. Keep your eye on Breeding.

PEEL. On Mr. Breeding?

BLAKE. Breeding is the weather vane. Assalone is the junkyard dog.

PEEL. Mr. Breeding doesn't have any real power.

BLAKE. He doesn't have power. He has *sway*.

PEEL. Sway is power, isn't it?

BLAKE. The ability to affect outcomes in a vacuum. That's power. But to affect *others*. That's sway.

PEEL. Blake, I never actually know what you're talking about.

BLAKE. If you bring up Carp and Assalone pounces on you, then you know they're lying in wait.

PEEL. *Who* is?

BLAKE. The whole faction. The *majority*. All of them.

PEEL. Wait a minute, aren't *you* one of them? Aren't we all in this together?

BLAKE. One thing you might have noticed about me is that I am extremely flexible. It won't help to get up on your soapbox.

PEEL. I don't have a soapbox.

BLAKE. Righteous indignation is a cheap perfume. Anybody can gin that up. This is realpolitik.

PEEL. I don't think you're saying that right.

BLAKE. What happens here today will have an impact for a long time to come.

PEEL. You think?

BLAKE. No. I don't know. It could.

PEEL. You've been drinking.

BLAKE. What's your point?

> (**MAYOR SUPERBA** *raps four times with his gavel.*)

SUPERBA. Good evening and welcome to a rainy night in Big Cherry. This is a good day. I want to thank everyone for coming to this closed session of the Big Cherry City Council. As we do the people's work. And so we're going to start tonight. Madam Clerk, will you please call the roll.

JOHNSON. Mr. Assalone.

ASSALONE. Assalone, here.

JOHNSON. Mr. Blake.

BLAKE. Here.

JOHNSON. Mr. Breeding.

BREEDING. Here.

JOHNSON. Mr. Carp.

> (*Silence.*)

My bad. Mr. Hanratty.

HANRATTY. Here.

JOHNSON. Ms. Innes.

INNES. Here.

JOHNSON. Ms. Matz.

MATZ. Here.

JOHNSON. Mr. Oldfield.

OLDFIELD. Here.

JOHNSON. Mr. Peel.

PEEL. Here.

JOHNSON. Mayor Superba.

SUPERBA. Here.

JOHNSON. We have a quorum.

SUPERBA. Thank you. Normally when we hold a closed meeting, we dispense with the invocation, but I'm going to ask Councilman Peel to lead us in prayer tonight. Mr. Peel?

PEEL. You want *me* to?

SUPERBA. If you're up for it.

(**ALL** *stand.*)

PEEL. Lord? We're very thankful for all of our blessings. Thank you for the rain and...thank you for all the people working tonight, our firemen and police officers, all of our first responders, and those who work for the city, and everyone who helps us to live, here in Big Cherry, to live and to work, with one another. Thank you to all who volunteer and make our town safe and healthy and. This rain, we've had a lot of rain, and sometimes we think maybe it's too much, it soaks the ground, and floods the lowlands. But, uh...rain is good, it's a good thing, the rain is a reminder of you and the things you provide for us. Pray for us, pray that we can be a good example. Amen.

ALL. Amen.

SUPERBA. Thank you. Yes, the rain.

(*That hangs for a moment.*)

And thanks also to our football team, the Savages, those kids are strong and talented and they've sure given us a lot to cheer about. I know we all look forward to Friday nights around here, and we're just so grateful to have that in our lives. They sure did a number on Grassland last Friday and I know we all enjoyed that. So now we'll pledge our allegiance.

> *(All **MEMBERS** face the flag, place their hands over their hearts.)*

ALL. I pledge allegiance

To the flag

Of the United States of America

And to the Republic

For which it stands

One nation

Under God

Indivisible

With liberty

And justice for all.

> *(They take their seats.)*

> *(Lights in the room flicker, dim, then buzz back full. **PEEL** seems to be the only one who takes note.)*

SUPERBA. Before we begin, any announcements?

OLDFIELD. I have an announcement.

SUPERBA. All right, go ahead.

OLDFIELD. Well, let's talk about parking.

SUPERBA. Is that an announcement?

OLDFIELD. I'm announcing that I'd like to talk about parking.

SUPERBA. George, that's not an announcement.

OLDFIELD. I believe it is.

SUPERBA. Announcing what you'd like to talk about is not an announcement, anymore than announcing that you're going to the bathroom.

OLDFIELD. Well, that's embarrassing. I didn't think when I came in here tonight I would have to hear the word "bathroom."

SUPERBA. That might not be the last time tonight you hear that word.

OLDFIELD. Let me go on the record as saying, "I hope it is."

SUPERBA. Are there any other announcements?

OLDFIELD. I would like to announce that there is an unclaimed empty parking space available to this council.

SUPERBA. What are you saying, that you want the parking space?

OLDFIELD. No, I'm not saying that. Even though I most definitely want the parking space. My announcement concerns the simple fact that a parking space that has been reserved for many many years has now become available and I don't recall that we've ever had a method in place for selecting the new...parker.

SUPERBA. I still don't consider this even remotely in the realm of "announcements." It certainly doesn't square with the nature of every other announcement we've read aloud in my sixteen years on the board.

OLDFIELD. Sixteen years, Mayor Superba? Sixteen, is that right?

SUPERBA. Something like that.

OLDFIELD. Because I have been on this board now for thirty-nine years, and let me tell you –

ASSALONE. Come on, George.

OLDFIELD. Now you wait a second, I get to finish this whatever this is.

ASSALONE. What is this?

OLDFIELD. It is what I set out to make. It is an announcement that a parking place, heretofore occupied, has now come free, and I think we have an obligation to determine the process for selecting the new occupier of the parking place. Space.

ASSALONE. Then why are you telling us how many years you've served on the board? That's not germane.

OLDFIELD. Well, I was responding to Mayor Superba's claim that he had never before heard an announcement like mine in his sixteen years on the board, and I was making the point that I've served on the board somewhat longer than that. But vis-a-vis the parking space allocation, it's also germane that no member of this board has served longer than I, and in fact no one really comes close except for Ms. Innes, and does anyone on this board find it strange that no one on this board parks further away than me? Farther?

ASSALONE. I don't find that strange. Does anyone else find that strange?

SUPERBA. I don't find it strange.

BREEDING. I don't find it strange.

OLDFIELD. Why don't you find it strange?

BREEDING. Why does anyone not find something strange?

OLDFIELD. That's no answer. Why don't *you* find it strange?

ASSALONE. Because nobody cares.

OLDFIELD. That has nothing to do with why it isn't strange!

SUPERBA. So you're saying it's not strange.

OLDFIELD. *You* said it's not strange.

SUPERBA. So we agree. Any other announcements?

OLDFIELD. Is this issue resolved? Rather, this issue is not resolved.

SUPERBA. Why don't you bring it up as new business at next week's meeting?

OLDFIELD. How can it be new business next week?

SUPERBA. Then bring it up as last week's business. Next week.

OLDFIELD. Might I bring it up as new business at *this* week's meeting?

SUPERBA. You might.

OLDFIELD. I might.

SUPERBA. Yes, now if there are no –

OLDFIELD. And I might not.

> *(Pause.)*

SUPERBA. If there are no further announcements, we can proceed with the approval of the minutes.

INNES. Your Honor, before we approve the minutes, I wonder if I might read something to the council.

> *(Some barely concealed groans and sighs from other* **MEMBERS.***)*

SUPERBA. And what is that?

INNES. A statement.

SUPERBA. What is the nature of the statement?

INNES. It is a statement I'd like to read to the council. About the council.

BREEDING. I wonder if it might be more appropriate to read in a meeting of the Council Rules Committee.

SUPERBA. Ms. Matz?

> *(Surprised to be called on, **MATZ** stands, spills some pills and pill bottles from a plastic bag.)*

MATZ. Yes?

SUPERBA. You're chairperson of the Council Rules Committee.

MATZ. Yes, I am.

SUPERBA. Is there a committee meeting scheduled in the near future?

MATZ. That would depend on your definition of future.

SUPERBA. "Events that will happen in the time to come."

MATZ. Then yes, of course.

SUPERBA. Ms. Innes?

INNES. All due respect, my piece doesn't address council rules, per se. It has more to do with spirit.

BREEDING. Spirit in what sense?

INNES. Esprit de corps.

BREEDING. Couldn't you just summarize the piece?

INNES. I could, but I don't think it would do the piece justice.

BREEDING. Does the piece deserve justice?

INNES. Don't all pieces?

BREEDING. No.

INNES. I write better than I speak.

BREEDING. Most of us write better than we speak but that doesn't mean we go around reading pre-written statements aloud.

INNES. Maybe *you* don't.

BREEDING. You do?

INNES. When permitted.

BREEDING. Are you often permitted?

INNES. I am occasionally permitted.

ASSALONE. For God's sake, just let her read it.

SUPERBA. All right, Ms. Innes, go ahead.

INNES. "To my fellow councilmembers and conscientious citizens of Big Cherry,

It's been my great pleasure to serve on this council for thirty-three-and-a-half years, thirty-five if you count my leave of absence. I have watched this board grow from a quaint and orderly group of six committed, unfailingly polite, and perhaps even timid villagers to the rowdy and robust democracy we now enjoy. Sure, over the years, we've had our dust-ups and differences, tête-à-têtes over policy, clashes of personalities, to say nothing of a certain rape and subsequent abortion, but that's all water under the bridge. Though the former mayor served no jail time, he lived out his days in sober disgrace, a Big Cherry pariah. All in all though, we as a governing body have had a successful tenure, measured as only these things can be: by the continued health, safety, and prosperity of our constituency. But now we find ourselves faced with a crisis of confidence that is perhaps the greatest challenge ever to the morale of our collective.

The events of last week's meeting still loom large for every member here, I'm sure. I know that, as individuals, each one of us holds a slightly different perspective on Mr. Carp and his fate, and each of us is certainly entitled to that perspective –"

SUPERBA. Ms. Innes –

INNES. I was led to believe I'd be allowed to speak my piece without interruption.

SUPERBA. I'm not sure who led you to believe that.

INNES. It was implicit in your instruction to proceed.

SUPERBA. Be that as it may, I would prefer if you eliminated any references to last week's meeting and simply told us what it is you intend to say.

BREEDING. Yes, let's cut to the chase.

INNES. My piece contains no chase.

BREEDING. Maybe your piece could use a chase.

INNES. May I continue?

SUPERBA. Yes. Sorry to interrupt.

INNES. *(Skimming through.)* Okay… "intense feelings… loyalty… ruled by fiat… long gray wet winter… pepper jelly…" Here we go, "On my first day as a councilmember, freshly scrubbed and wide-eyed with innocence, I was told we were given one responsibility that outstripped all others – no matter that the man who told me would later force himself on me in a drunken psychotic rage. That regardless of how badly we might bungle the distribution and management of services and funds, no matter how much we might waste our community's time and money and goods and services, regardless of how crooked and slimy and subhuman we might be as individuals, that above all else the prime responsibility of this civic organ is the loving care and firm management of the Big Cherry Heritage Festival."

BREEDING. Hear, hear.

INNES. "There is no event, no document, no motto or creed, indeed no person more important to the preservation of our civic mission than this festival. It is the pride of our city, our state, our people. In short, it is who we are. I suggest that we take a moment to reflect on the meaning of November 29, 1872. I suggest for all of us, from the most weathered veteran…" That's you, George.

OLDFIELD. Yes.

INNES. "...From the most weathered veteran to our most jejune amateur..." That's you, Mr. Peel.

PEEL. Not sure you're saying that right.

INNES. *(Maintaining her mispronunciation.)* "...*Jejune amateur*, we take a moment of silence to honor the fallen and the sacrifices they made so that we may live as we now do: in safety and comfort, surrounded by our families and friends, with health insurance and ripe fruit, and a hopeful tear in our eye."

    (Pause.)

BREEDING. Thank you for that, Ms. Innes –

SUPERBA. Moment of silence.

BREEDING. Right.

    (A moment of silence.)

INNES. Thank you.

SUPERBA. Now can we please take –

INNES. *(Continues reading.)* "And with that shared moment, I hope that we find –"

SUPERBA. Ms. Innes. Is the moment of silence not the conclusion of your piece?

INNES. Not quite.

SUPERBA. The moment of silence traditionally concludes a piece.

INNES. Clearly my piece is untraditional.

BREEDING. I object.

INNES. You object?

BREEDING. I do.

INNES. Am I on trial? Do I need to avail myself of a lawyer?

BREEDING. I won't be held hostage.

INNES. I'll inform your family.

SUPERBA. Carry on, Ms. Innes.

INNES. "And with that shared moment..." The shared moment I refer to here is the moment of silence.

SUPERBA. Yes.

INNES. "And with that shared moment, I hope that we find ourselves with a shared feeling. A shared conviction. That what we have done is *right*. That we do what we do for the greater *good*. That we as a group have faced a test in which we might have put the interests of one man above the common weal but we instead rose to the moment –"

SUPERBA. Ms. Innes?

INNES. Yes.

SUPERBA. Your piece is now finished.

INNES. But Mr. Mayor, I was just at the point wherein I summarize the superiority of our –

SUPERBA. Ms. Innes. Your piece is finished.

INNES. *(Quietly.)* Thank you.

> *(An awkward silence. Shuffle of papers. Subtle flicker of the lights.)*

SUPERBA. So we're ready to begin the meeting with the approval of the minutes. At this time, are there any corrections, deletions, or additions to the minutes as they were presented? If not, I'll ask for a motion to approve the minutes.

BREEDING. So moved.

ASSALONE. Second.

SUPERBA. I have a motion by Councilman Breeding and a second by Councilman Assalone to approve the minutes as they were presented. Is there any discussion? If not, we're ready to vote.

PEEL. Um, yes, I'm sorry. I see the minutes for the October eighteenth meeting but are there no minutes for the October twenty-fifth meeting?

SUPERBA. The motion concerns the minutes you have in your folder.

PEEL. I understand.

BREEDING. Boilerplate.

PEEL. Right, I just thought we got the minutes from the last meeting at the next meeting. Meaning I would have thought the minutes from the October eighteenth meeting would have been distributed at the October twenty-fifth meeting and that the minutes for the October twenty-fifth meeting would be distributed tonight.

SUPERBA. I understand your question, Mr. Peel. It would appear that the minutes for the meeting in question have not yet been prepared for distribution and so we'll have to wait until the next meeting to review those minutes.

PEEL. I understand.

SUPERBA. So if there is no further discussion, we might vote? Madam Clerk?

JOHNSON. Mr. Assalone.

ASSALONE. Assalone. Yes.

PEEL. I'm sorry, just one moment before we continue the vote.

ASSALONE. We're voting.

PEEL. But before we continue. I'm curious, the minutes missing in this way, is that uncommon?

SUPERBA. The minutes are not missing, Mr. Peel, they are simply delayed.

PEEL. Right. And is that uncommon?

SUPERBA. I couldn't speak to how common that is.

PEEL. Can anyone? Mr. Oldfield?

OLDFIELD. What? What are you asking me for?

PEEL. You've been on the council the longest. I thought maybe you could answer how common it is for the minutes to be delayed.

OLDFIELD. I don't make it a habit to sit around conjecturing about what is common or uncommon.

PEEL. I'm sure you don't, but in this one instance, could you tell me if it's uncommon for the minutes to be delayed?

OLDFIELD. Don't pick on me!

PEEL. For heaven's sake, let me just put the question to the group. Can anyone here tell me if it is uncommon for the minutes of a meeting to be delayed?

(No one speaks.)

ASSALONE. Apparently not.

SUPERBA. We can continue the vote.

JOHNSON. Mr. Blake.

BLAKE. Yes.

JOHNSON. Mr. Breeding.

PEEL. Ms. Johnson.

BREEDING. Wait.

PEEL. Ms. Johnson, can *you* say?

BREEDING. She's asked me for my vote.

PEEL. I know but I'm just trying to ascertain why the minutes from last week's meeting –

BREEDING. But you can't speak. When she asks for my vote, she is waiting for me to speak. We are all waiting for me to speak.

PEEL. I'm sorry.

BREEDING. *(To* **JOHNSON**.*)* Yes.

PEEL. Ms. Johnson.

SUPERBA. She is taking the vote, Mr. Peel.

PEEL. I'd like to continue the discussion. Just for a moment.

BREEDING. This is all boilerplate.

PEEL. Ms. Johnson, can you tell me why the minutes are delayed?

SUPERBA. Mr. Peel.

PEEL. Can you?

BREEDING. Mr. Mayor, point of order.

SUPERBA. Really, Mr. Peel, we should continue the voting process. Ms. Johnson.

JOHNSON. Mr. Carp.

(Silence.)

My bad. Mr. Hanratty.

HANRATTY. Yes.

JOHNSON. Ms. Innes.

INNES. Yes.

JOHNSON. Ms. Matz.

MATZ. Here. I mean yes.

JOHNSON. Mr. Oldfield.

OLDFIELD. Yes.

JOHNSON. Mr. Peel.

PEEL. Ms. Johnson? Can you answer my question?

BREEDING. Point of order!

PEEL. I'm just trying to learn where the minutes for last week's meeting have got to.

ASSALONE. *Got* to. Who says they *got* to anywhere?

PEEL. Mr. Mayor, I'm simply asking if not having the minutes from the previous week's meeting has ever happened before.

SUPERBA. Yes, it's happened before. Happened last week.

PEEL. Thank you.

JOHNSON. *(To* **SUPERBA***.)* Can I get on with the vote?

PEEL. I vote yes.

BREEDING. Ah.

JOHNSON. Mayor Superba.

SUPERBA. Yes.

JOHNSON. The motion carries.

SUPERBA. The motion carries and the minutes are approved as presented. We now move to Item 6.1 and this item concerns recovered lost or stolen bicycles.

PEEL. I'm sorry, quick question. I know this item came to the council's attention due to the work of Mr. Carp and I'm a little flummoxed to find him absent from this meeting today and I really hate to discuss the item on the agenda without him here.

SUPERBA. Mr. Carp is no longer on the council, Mr. Peel.

PEEL. Yes, I heard that, I was told that, but absent a copy of the minutes, I'm a little unclear as to why that is. And I'd like to at least follow up on this agenda item in a way that would suit Mr. Carp. He came to learn that the Sheriff's Department was recovering more than a hundred lost and stolen bicycles each year, on the streets of Big Cherry and the greater metropolitan Big Cherry area, and that Sheriff Assalone, Councilman Assalone's brother, was holding them in police storage and then disposing of them. So Mr. Carp activated a search for charitable organizations to which Sheriff Assalone could donate these bikes. Troubled teens' youth shelter, and the Lutheran Church, and a couple of others.

(*Beat.*)

Maybe some of you know this, but again, I missed the last meeting and I don't have a copy of the minutes and Mr. Carp isn't here to inform me about the direction he would want me to take this.

ASSALONE. You missed a meeting.

PEEL. Yes, I missed last week's meeting –

ASSALONE. *You* missed a meeting. And so now you expect us to use the time in this week's meeting to inform you about last week's meeting. As if that's the best use of our time.

PEEL. Um. You wouldn't need... No one would need to catch me up if I had a copy of the minutes from last week's meeting.

ASSALONE. But those minutes do not exist. You've been told that and now you're holding up the meeting to get someone to recite to you what happened at last week's meeting. That you missed.

PEEL. You keep saying that, Mr. Assalone. I know I missed the meeting, I was at my mother's deathbed and subsequent funeral.

ASSALONE. And while I'm sure everyone here feels great sympathy for your loss, it's not our fault that your mother is dead.

PEEL. No...it's not...

SUPERBA. Mr. Peel, if it helps: this item has been resolved in a way that I believe Mr. Carp would have found more than satisfactory.

BREEDING. *More* than satisfactory.

SUPERBA. Sheriff Assalone has agreed to donate the bikes to the nonprofit which shows the greatest need. A portion to the youth shelter, a portion to the Lutheran Church and so on. Right, Mr. Assalone?

ASSALONE. Oh sure. Gratis.

PEEL. Great.

ASSALONE. Write-off.

PEEL. Well, that's great to hear.

SUPERBA. *(To the group.)* So there's no need for further discussion on Item 6.1, is there? Ms. Matz?

MATZ. Yes, no, there is no need for further discussion. God knows.

SUPERBA. Right, but in light of Mr. Carp's absence, you might recall I asked you to write up the resolution so that we could vote on it.

MATZ. Yes, my recollection is that you asked me to write up the resolution so that we could vote on it.

SUPERBA. That's my recollection.

MATZ. Mine too. But the *truth* is…the *truth* is, I haven't done that.

SUPERBA. Okay.

MATZ. And I'm not sure why. Remind me, what resolution is this?

SUPERBA. The resolution stipulates that Sheriff Assalone will donate the bicycles to the nonprofit that shows the greatest need.

MATZ. Yes, of course. I understand.

SUPERBA. Okay. Will you do it?

MATZ. Yes. What.

SUPERBA. Write up the resolution.

MATZ. Yes.

SUPERBA. For next week?

MATZ. *(Long, unmotivated pause.)* Yes.

SUPERBA. All right, so we can move on to our next item, 7.1. The Fountain at Mackie Creek Park. Mr. Hanratty, you have the floor.

HANRATTY. Yes, I would like to discuss the fountain.

BREEDING. *(Sotto voce.)* Here we go.

HANRATTY. Here we go: So, just so you understand, I've had some visual aids drawn up.

> (**HANRATTY** *gets the posters he entered with, erects them on an easel. The top one is a very simple, large outline map.* **HANRATTY** *uses a laser pointer for his presentation.*)

Just to orient you. This is City Hall. This is the old Rexall Drug. Right? Here's the battlefield. Mackie Creek, of course. And right here is the current fountain.

OLDFIELD. Now Harry, what am I looking at here? Is this a medallion?

HANRATTY. What? A medallion?

OLDFIELD. Is this a medallion of some sort, a hood ornament? It spins with the wind, that sort of thing?

HANRATTY. No, George. It's...it's a *map*. Of the park.

OLDFIELD. Got it.

HANRATTY. You know this fountain. People without disabilities are able to walk up to it, up those old circular stone steps, and sit on the edge, have an ice cream. Some throw in coins.

OLDFIELD. And what is the purpose of those coins?

HANRATTY. What?

OLDFIELD. To what end do they put coins in the fountain?

HANRATTY. To make a wish.

OLDFIELD. The wishes cost money?

HANRATTY. Uh.

ASSALONE. For God's sake, George.

OLDFIELD. What?

ASSALONE. You aren't familiar with the tradition of tossing a coin in a fountain and making a wish?

OLDFIELD. Excuse me, friends, I'll shut up!

HANRATTY. In any case, people without disabilities have an access to the fountain that the disabled have simply never enjoyed. And that's unfair.

OLDFIELD. *(To* **ASSALONE.***)* And I suppose you know what happens to all those coins too, smart guy!

INNES. You've spit on me, George.

OLDFIELD. Sorry.

INNES. My God, you've spit on me.

OLDFIELD. I'm sorry.

SUPERBA. Can you explain why I have two sets of numbers here?

HANRATTY. Certainly, Mr. Mayor. If you look in your folder, you'll see the green-shaded pages, and these show the financial proposal for a complete renovation of the fountain, in which we rip out the old one and replace it completely with a majestic new fountain, designed by local architect Faint Waysbury.

SUPERBA. And the pink-shaded pages?

HANRATTY. That's the less expensive option. I'll be honest and tell you I'm not as fond of it, it's far less aesthetically pleasing and it feels like a stopgap solution.

SUPERBA. Which is...?

HANRATTY. Uh, a plank. It's...it's just a plank, it allows anyone in a wheelchair to roll up the plank to the fountain.

SUPERBA. It's substantially less money.

BREEDING. Lot less money.

HANRATTY. It is. It's a plank.

BREEDING. You know, a plank has other practical applications. It could be used, for instance, for large industrial equipment to roll directly to the fountain.

HANRATTY. The fountain does not require large industrial equipment.

BREEDING. Really? There isn't some kind of large industrial equipment that might be used to repair the fountain or perform some other kind of maintenance?

HANRATTY. I wouldn't know what that is.

BREEDING. I thought you were going to research this project.

HANRATTY. I've done substantial research.

BREEDING. And yet you can't tell us the purpose of large industrial equipment accessing the fountain by this plank?

HANRATTY. No, Mr. Breeding, I can't, because there's no reason large industrial equipment would need to get to the fountain and what's more, I don't know what large industrial equipment you're referring to.

BREEDING. Because you haven't done enough research.

OLDFIELD. You could use that plank to dolly out all those coins.

HANRATTY. Not enough coins accumulate to warrant the use of a dolly.

OLDFIELD. So this plank is superfluous.

HANRATTY. No, the purpose of the plank is so that my sister, or any other soul confined to the use of a wheelchair, can reach the fountain and see the bottom of it!

OLDFIELD. There's nothing so interesting about the bottom of it.

HANRATTY. There is if you've never seen it!

OLDFIELD. Bring your sister around, I can assure her there's not much to see at the bottom of a fountain.

INNES. You could just show her a picture.

(Pause.)

HANRATTY. Mr. Mayor, I'd like to show the council a rendering of the fountain, should we choose the more complete renovation.

> *(**HANRATTY** displays the second poster, a rendering of a public fountain. An ornate statue of an American soldier, circa 1872, in battle, on horseback, occupies the center of the fountain. Other **MEMBERS** nod, coo their approval.)*

As you see: the grounds, the battlefield. And just to orient you, the old Rexall Drug would be over here. The fountain is positioned in the center of our mall, and I believe it should help, through architecture and landscaping, tell a narrative about OW!

(Picks something off his neck.)

HANRATTY. Sorry, Jesus, I got bit by an ant. Uh, the fountain should help through architecture and landscaping tell a narrative about our community and the people who created it. Providing a majestic view of the battlefield, this new fountain would become the emotional centerpiece of our park and our community. More to the point, it would be completely accessible by everyone. And, as should be evident from the rendering, this new bronze statue provides a dramatic explanation point to the story of Big Cherry.

BLAKE. Exclamation point.

HANRATTY. What?

BLAKE. You said "*explanation* point."

HANRATTY. I don't think so.

BLAKE. Yes you did.

HANRATTY. Okay, thanks.

OLDFIELD. Now friends, I fully expect you're going to throw me on the floor and kick me in the face, but I assure you I have no idea what is happening. Does any of this actually exist?

ASSALONE. No.

OLDFIELD. Very good.

BLAKE. *Who* is the architect?

HANRATTY. Faint Waysbury. She's local.

BLAKE. What else has she done?

HANRATTY. She did a fountain very similar to this one, though of a smaller scale, at the junior college in Grassland.

BLAKE. Nice.

HANRATTY. Do you know that fountain?

BLAKE. No.

INNES. Who did the drawing?

HANRATTY. Faint.

INNES. What?

HANRATTY. *Faint.*

INNES. *(To* **OLDFIELD.***)* What is he saying?

OLDFIELD. Not sure.

HANRATTY. *Faint Waysbury.* The architect.

OLDFIELD. Is she a very tall woman?

HANRATTY. No.

OLDFIELD. I mean *really* tall. Like seven feet.

HANRATTY. No.

OLDFIELD. I must have her confused with someone else. This *giant.*

HANRATTY. Are there any questions or comments about the proposal?

BREEDING. Mr. Hanratty, I'm sure we all appreciate your situation with your sister, but...how do I phrase this... isn't that just the way it is? I mean, aren't there certain things the disabled aren't able to do that able-bodied people *are* able to do?

HANRATTY. Like?

BREEDING. Well, like walk. "I am dis*abled* therefore I am not *able* to walk up to the fountain."

HANRATTY. That's very insensitive, Mr. Breeding.

BREEDING. There's no need for name-calling.

HANRATTY. I would argue that the whole point of my enterprise is to forge a community that is not only inclusive, but compassionate.

BREEDING. Right, but looking at the financials here, it seems like your compassion is going to cost the taxpayers a pretty penny. And I don't know that normal people should have to suffer an onerous tax burden just so your sister can wheel up to a fountain.

HANRATTY. "Normal people"?

BREEDING. Oh, here we go, the language police. You know what I mean.

HANRATTY. I think I do!

BREEDING. I just mean people who don't have anything wrong with them.

HANRATTY. Does anyone *else* care to comment on the proposal?

> (**HANRATTY** *tries and fails to make eye contact with* **PEEL**. *He tosses his proposal at* **PEEL***, getting his attention, and then urges* **PEEL** *to speak.*)

PEEL. Oh. Oh! I like the design and the statue and this picture is really pretty. And I certainly would stand up for...for people who can't. I appreciate the work Mr. Hanratty has put into this and I think it's a fine idea.

HANRATTY. Thank you, Mr. Poole.

PEEL. Peel.

HANRATTY. Peel.

PEEL. Just one question, who is the figure in the middle, the statue?

> (*A few laughs.*)

Sorry?

> (*Another laugh, dying out.*)

SUPERBA. You really don't know?

PEEL. Uhhh, what, is it obvious? Ulysses S. Grant, or...?

(And now a dark silence descends.)

Sorry, should I know it? It's...

SUPERBA. Are you not familiar with the Battle at Mackie Creek?

PEEL. Oh, yeah, he's, he's a figure from that? Historical figure from that?

SUPERBA. You don't know the story.

PEEL. Uh, I know there was quite a battle at Mackie Creek, during the Civil War, or...

INNES. Public education is a joke.

PEEL. You know what, I don't, clearly. I don't really know the whole story.

SUPERBA. "November 29, 1872."

(The **MEMBERS** *stand and perform a re-enactment of the Battle at Mackie Creek, accompanied by* **SUPERBA***'s narration.)*

"They say it was cold that day, bitterly cold for November, an early sign of a miserable winter to come. A small troupe of eight horse soldiers, led by Sergeant Otto Pym, had split from their division on a reconnaissance mission and on this night, they were billeted in the home of Mr. J. Farmer – coincidentally, a farmer."

BREEDING (FARMER). "You are more than welcome to bed in our house, Sergeant Pym, and your horses are surely welcome to our water. But what is the purpose of your mission? Your very presence has made me and my wife wary."

INNES (MRS. FARMER). "And our daughter Debbie is plainly scared."

ASSALONE (PYM). "There's been much activity from the Sioux in this area, Mr. Farmer. We've had many reports of stables burned and horses thieved. Farmers and trappers clear from here to Grassland have made report of skirmishes and the like. And while I like not to scare your daughter Debbie, it is true that the Sioux put a store in white children, particularly young girls."

SUPERBA. "The whole of the Farmer family bedded down in the parents' room, while four of the men slept in the room of the Farmers' daughter Debbie. The other four soldiers slept in the hayloft. Sergeant Otto Pym slept with his men in the barn, for he was the sort of soldier who insisted that no man under his command would suffer more hardship than he. A November wind in this country can be mistaken for many things, even the devil himself, so the soldiers could be forgiven for dismissing the early signs of the stealthy Sioux."

(**OLDFIELD** *hoots.*)

And indeed it was not a *sound* that alerted Sergeant Pym to the Sioux's attack...but a smell."

ASSALONE (PYM). "What's that smell? Stanton! Are you smoking a cigar? What the – FIRE! SIOUX!"

(**OLDFIELD** *crinkles paper to create the sound of fire.*)

SUPERBA. "The dry hay of winter ignited like nitro! The soldiers in the hayloft awoke to the horror of their bedroom barn engulfed in flames!"

(**MEMBERS** *scream.*)

ASSALONE (PYM). "Save the Farmers!"

SUPERBA. "Pym flew out of the hayloft and literally ran through fire, blindly charging into the smoky night where he was set upon by a young Sioux warrior!"

(**ASSALONE** *grapples with* **HANRATTY.**)

"Around them, chaos reigned! Twenty Sioux warriors torched the Farmers' home, rounded up the Farmers' horses, and shot every white man in sight indiscriminately, civilian and soldier alike, with long rifles as well as the bow and arrow. Pym, struggling valiantly with his young savage, saw his best soldier, young Archibald Stanton, shot in the back while running for the Farmer house."

*(**ASSALONE** overcomes **HANRATTY**.)*

"Finally, Pym overcame his adversary and took up a vantage point behind the Farmers' well. Using the young warrior's long gun, he began to pick off the marauders with remarkable sharp-shooting. One, then two, then four, then five. The Sioux realized they were being decimated by a lone sniper and so they approached the well. That only made them easier to see, and to shoot! Now Pym had picked off ten, now twelve! The savages had their fill, and they had their horses, and they called out for a retreat. The remaining Sioux gathered themselves and thundered off into the night. And Sergeant Pym was able to approach the half-burned Farmer house."

*(**ASSALONE** approaches **BREEDING**.)*

ASSALONE (PYM). "Mr. Farmer, they're gone! They've done in your barn and they've stolen your horses but your crops survive. I've lost many of my men. Is your family hurt?"

BREEDING (FARMER). "DEBBIE! They've stolen my daughter! They've stolen my beautiful daughter and now we'll never see her again!"

INNES (MRS. FARMER). "They will rape her and raise her as one of their own! It is a fate worse than any death!"

SUPERBA. "But Mrs. Farmer's sentence was not complete before Sergeant Pym was on horseback and riding after the Sioux."

(**ASSALONE** *gallops off on an imaginary horse.*)

SUPERBA. "The Farmers began to put their shattered lives back together. They covered the dead soldiers and dressed the wounded. They saved what they could from the smoldering embers of their barn and house. And in the first light of a frigid dawn, they had nearly collapsed from exhaustion...when they heard the clop-clop of horse hooves."

BREEDING (FARMER). "I swear, Mother, I might be asleep and dreaming. Or I might be dead. But tell me, please tell me, do you see it too?"

(**ASSALONE** *re-enters, carrying* **MATZ.**)

SUPERBA. "Sergeant Otto Pym rode onto that homestead. He got down from his horse and walked to Mr. and Mrs. Farmer with little Debbie Farmer in his outstretched arms. He handed their daughter to them and said..."

ASSALONE (PYM). "Here is your future."

SUPERBA. "And as soon as they had taken Debbie from him, he collapsed to the ground...with three arrows protruding from his back. And the town of Big Cherry was saved."

ALL. "And the town of Big Cherry was saved."

(**ALL** *stare at* **PEEL.**)

PEEL. Wow. Wow, that's...quite a story. Wow.

SUPERBA. "And the town of Big Cherry was saved."

PEEL. Yeah, wow. That's...you know, it's interesting but the Natalie Wood character in *The Searchers*, Natalie Wood gets kidnapped by Indians, and her name is Debbie.

SUPERBA. Deborah Farmer grew to be an important figure in this town. Almost like royalty.

PEEL. Oh yeah?

SUPERBA. Land holdings, oil and real estate. Tremendous wealth.

PEEL. Really, that's really…

SUPERBA. "Here is your future."

> *(The **MEMBERS** now return to their seats.)*

PEEL. Yeah, wow, he really said that. With three arrows in his back, that's quite a…quite an achievement.

> *(**ALL** continue to stare at **PEEL**. Some smiles, some nods.)*

Quite an achievement. My wife is from here, it's weird she never told me that. That's really some, that's…vivid.

> *(Turns his attention to the rendering.)*

And so the statue here is the guy from the story.

SUPERBA. Sergeant Otto Pym.

PEEL. Otto Pym, right, I wonder why they didn't name the town Pymville or Pym Town or Pymsylvania. I mean, why Big Cherry, there aren't any cherry trees around here.

ALL. *(Some mumbled paraphrased version of:)* I think there used to be cherry trees.

PEEL. So this is Otto Pym crashing the Sioux party to get back Little Debbie.

HANRATTY. Yes, and right here, at the base of the fountain, there would be a ribbon. Not an actual ribbon, a ribbon of stone, and it says…

HANRATTY.	**SUPERBA**.
"And the town of Big Cherry was saved."	"Here is your future."

HANRATTY. Uh, no, it says, "And the town of Big Cherry was saved."

SUPERBA. It should say, "Here is your future."

HANRATTY. You're right. It should. "Here is your future." Mr. Mayor, I request an up-or-down vote on my complete renovation.

SUPERBA. Very well. We'll vote on Agenda Item 7.1, Mr. Hanratty's Resolution to Design and Build an Accessible Fountain. Madam Clerk?

JOHNSON. Mr. Assalone.

ASSALONE. Assalone, no.

JOHNSON. Mr. Blake.

BLAKE. No.

JOHNSON. Mr. Breeding.

BREEDING. No.

JOHNSON. Mr…

(*Beat.*)

Mr. Hanratty.

HANRATTY. Yes.

JOHNSON. Ms. Innes.

INNES. No.

JOHNSON. Ms. Matz.

(*No response.*)

Ms. Matz.

MATZ. Sorry, no.

JOHNSON. Mr. Oldfield.

OLDFIELD. No.

JOHNSON. Mr. Peel.

PEEL. Yes.

JOHNSON. Mayor Superba.

SUPERBA. No.

JOHNSON. Seven votes no, two votes yes. The resolution fails to pass.

OLDFIELD. *(Taking items from a Tupperware container.)* Say, whatever happened to that old Rexall Drug, anyway? That was a fine store. I used to go in there at lunchtime and get a lime-aid in a Styrofoam cup and a little package of cheese crackers.

INNES. It became the CVS.

OLDFIELD. The *what*?

INNES. The CVS drugstore.

> *(**OLDFIELD** looks stricken.)*

HANRATTY. Mr. Mayor, I'm perplexed by your resistance. I thought the statue of Pym… especially given last week's meeting –

SUPERBA. The statue is simply spectacular.

BREEDING. *Great* statue. Come back to us when it's *just* the statue. 'Cause this accessible fountain? Bit of a reach.

> *(**BREEDING** tosses Hanratty's proposal into a trash can.)*

HANRATTY. *(Pained.)* A *reach*, it's…it's the entire point of the project…

OLDFIELD. *(Misty and forlorn.)* My God. Cheese crackers.

INNES. *(Oh, give it a rest.)* They sell cheese crackers at the CVS.

BLAKE. Mr. Mayor, I'd like to offer some assistance to my esteemed colleague. And in fact, it's the next item on our agenda, so if I may…?

SUPERBA. Yes, Item 7.2, "Lincoln Smackdown." You have the floor, Mr. Blake.

BLAKE. I mentioned last week at the meeting of the Big Cherry Heritage Festival Planning Committee this notion I had for an income-generating enterprise. Originally I had thought we would use it only temporarily for the festival, just a makeshift tent, much in the tradition of an attraction you might find at the state fair.

INNES. Like a freak show!

BLAKE. Yes, I suppose –

INNES. Oh I used to love the freaks. I remember this one man they advertised as the Missing Link. In reality, he was just this sad little man with misshapen feet dressed in a loincloth, sitting in a cardboard box. I never laughed so hard!

OLDFIELD. I don't remember that but it *sounds* funny.

BREEDING. *(Loud whisper.)* Careful, the PC police are out in force!

INNES. Say no m-o-r-e.

HANRATTY. I know how to spell "more."

BLAKE. I think now that Lincoln Smackdown might become a permanent fixture of the park. Essentially, Lincoln Smackdown is an opportunity for anyone to fight Honest Abe in a steel cage. We take a trained mixed martial arts fighter and dress him up as Abraham Lincoln. Shenandoah, black suit, stovepipe hat.

INNES. I love Abraham Lincoln. And violence.

OLDFIELD. You should get that giant lady to play Abraham Lincoln, she will scare the shit out of you.

HANRATTY. Mr. Mayor, I'm a little confused as to why we are hearing a proposal for Lincoln Smackdown when we just heard it last week. Are we supposed to vote on Lincoln Smackdown at every meeting?

BLAKE. I'm trying to *help* you, Harry. I think we should just add one dollar to every Lincoln Smackdown ticket and that's a way to pay for your fountain.

HANRATTY. First of all, Blake, I appreciate your help, but I have to be honest and tell you that I can't see Lincoln Smackdown generating the revenue to pay for itself, much less to pay for the accessible fountain. And secondly, I find Lincoln Smackdown a deeply offensive idea and so does anyone else who is a person of conscience. Beyond being dumb and offensive, its point of reference is obscure; did Lincoln ever visit Big Cherry? Did he ever discuss it? Do we know if he was even *aware* of it?

BLAKE. If there's one lesson the Civil War taught us, it's that Lincoln was aware of *all* of America.

HANRATTY. That doesn't mean he has anything to do with our town.

BLAKE. He was the Father of Our Country!

HANRATTY. George Washington was the Father of Our Country, nimrod.

BLAKE. So now Lincoln *wasn't* the Father of Our Country?

HANRATTY. He was the Great Emancipator!

BLAKE. *You* gonna tell *me* about the Great Emancipator?!

HANRATTY. The Great Emancipator didn't practice mixed martial arts!

BLAKE. Emancipate *this*, turkey!

> (**HANRATTY** *and* **BLAKE** *go at it.* **PEEL** *breaks them up.* **SUPERBA** *pounds his gavel.*)

SUPERBA. All right, all right, gentlemen, that's enough, calm down!

HANRATTY. Mr. Mayor, my question remains: Why are we required to go back over this territory? We covered Lincoln Smackdown last week.

BLAKE. We did not. We discussed it in the Planning Committee.

HANRATTY. And we threw it out! When we throw something out of the Planning Committee, that doesn't mean you then simply bring it before the board. That's the whole idea behind the Planning Committee. That's why we *have* a Planning Committee. That's why we have *any* committee. And I don't think we *did* just discuss this in the Planning Committee, I distinctly remember the topic of Lincoln Smackdown coming up in our general board meeting.

BLAKE. It did not!

HANRATTY. It did!

BLAKE. It did not!

HANRATTY. It did!

> *(They go back at each other, and again* **PEEL** *breaks it up.)*

SUPERBA. Gentlemen, there's an easy way to find out. Why don't we have a brief recess and we'll get to the bottom of this when we get back from break.

OLDFIELD. Thank God, I need to go to the terlet.

SUPERBA. Five minutes.

> *(***SUPERBA*** *raps his gavel. The* **MEMBERS** *stand, stretch their legs, get coffee, exit to the bathroom, etc.)*

> *(***HANRATTY*** *approaches* **PEEL.***)*

HANRATTY. Thanks for your help, Peel. These people are philistines.

PEEL. I think it's a fine idea, Mr. Hanratty. I'm sure you'll eventually get the support you need.

HANRATTY. I hope they all die in a fire.

> (**HANRATTY** *moves off.* **PEEL** *takes out his cellphone, dials.* **SUPERBA** *approaches, gives* **JOHNSON** *a handwritten note.*)

PEEL. *(Waiting on the phone.)* Spirited.

SUPERBA. What's that?

PEEL. It's a spirited group.

SUPERBA. Democracy's messy.

PEEL. I appreciate everyone's passion.

> (*As* **PEEL** *leaves his message,* **JOHNSON** *takes the note offstage.* **SUPERBA** *sharpens his pencil at Johnson's desk.*)

(Into phone.) Hi, Mr. Carp, it's me, Peel, Mr. Peel, Dr. Peel, it's Brian Peel, from the city council, will you do me a favor and give me a ring back, or a text, and give me some indication what in the world has happened? Everyone here is being very vague about last week's meeting and I'd just love to get it straight from the horse's mouth. We're just on a break right now but please, if you get a minute, call or text and tell me something. All right, hope you're well.

> (**PEEL** *hangs up.*)

SUPERBA. You have children, Mr. Peel?

PEEL. I have a daughter. Eighteen months.

> (**PEEL** *shows* **SUPERBA** *the iPhone photo.*)

SUPERBA. Oh she's great. What a sweetheart. That's a nice phone too, is that the new one?

PEEL. Yeah, I just got it. You, you have kids?

SUPERBA. Two boys. Teenagers.

PEEL. Oh!

SUPERBA. Couldn't be more different. Carter's the older one, very serious, very bookish, always reading. Very smart, very methodical. But a great weird sense of humor. Wants to be an animator. Can you believe that?

PEEL. Hm.

SUPERBA. No idea where that comes from. An *animator*. And then the youngest boy, Jake, just the opposite. Wild and explosive, this mercurial temper. Really fine athlete, just a terrific natural athlete. Nonstop energy.

PEEL. And were they like that as babies? Could you see that difference in them even then?

SUPERBA. Oh. Clearly. Carter would brood, and he was sick all the time. Drawing these elaborate mazes. I don't remember him eating anything other than peanut butter until he was ten. And Jake came out of the womb fast and never slowed down. Breaking everything in sight. Always in trouble.

>   (Lost in thought.)

It's really fascinating. They're both such fine young men. But their relationship to the world, to other people, just couldn't be any more different.

>   (Takes in **PEEL**, laughs.)

They drive you crazy too.

PEEL. Yeah, right?

SUPERBA. Hm. What's your daughter's name?

PEEL. Justine.

SUPERBA. That's a nice name.

(**SUPERBA** *puts his hand on* **PEEL***'s shoulder, looks him in the eye, smiles warmly.* **SUPERBA** *exits as* **JOHNSON** *re-enters.*)

(**OLDFIELD** *returns from the bathroom.*)

OLDFIELD. Listen to that rain. They'll have to build an ark to get us all out of here.

MATZ. Only two on the ark.

OLDFIELD. What's that?

MATZ. We don't all get on the ark. Two of every species. Only two of us get to go.

(**JOHNSON** *approaches* **PEEL**.)

JOHNSON. So I'm about to announce what I found out.

PEEL. Hm? What's that?

JOHNSON. If we discussed Lincoln Smackdown in last week's general meeting.

PEEL. Mr. Blake doesn't remember, I find that off-putting.

JOHNSON. You're missing the point.

PEEL. I think I'd know what I did and said last week.

SUPERBA. Ladies and gentlemen, if we could start to regroup.

(*The* **MEMBERS** *make their way back to their seats.*)

JOHNSON. And if you couldn't?

PEEL. If I couldn't?

JOHNSON. If you couldn't remember? What you did or said last week?

PEEL. You could always consult the...

(**PEEL** *has a realization.*)

JOHNSON. Wake up.

> (**MAYOR SUPERBA** *raps four times with the gavel.*)

SUPERBA. Our meeting is back in session. We were discussing Agenda Item 7.2, Mr. Blake's proposal for an attraction, perhaps permanent, perhaps a temporary attraction for the Big Cherry Heritage Festival. Madam Clerk, you were going to clarify for us if this agenda item was discussed at last week's general meeting?

JOHNSON. It was brought up in the general meeting though we never heard a formal proposal.

BLAKE. No, I didn't *submit* anything –

HANRATTY. That wasn't my point, I was saying that we had already –

PEEL. Excuse me, sorry, but can you tell me how we know this information? That it was brought up in the general meeting?

SUPERBA. Ms. Johnson has looked it up.

PEEL. Right, but looked it up in what?

SUPERBA. In her *notes*, Mr. Peel.

PEEL. And how are her notes different from the minutes?

ASSALONE. Oh my God, what is it with you?

PEEL. I beg your pardon?

ASSALONE. The minutes are not prepared for distribution. Why is that so difficult to grasp?

PEEL. Ms. Johnson, can you tell me if you merely have notes, or you have prepared minutes?

ASSALONE. She doesn't have to answer that.

PEEL. Why *wouldn't* she answer it?

ASSALONE. Because we've already been told that the minutes are not prepared for distribution.

PEEL. And I'd like to learn the impediment to their distribution.

ASSALONE. There is no impediment. That's like saying on Tuesday that Wednesday is the impediment to Thursday. They're not done yet.

PEEL. Mr. Assalone, I fail to see why this question is so vexing to you.

ASSALONE. Because you're wasting our time!

PEEL. Ms. Johnson, can you tell me –?

JOHNSON. The minutes are prepared. The minutes from last week are completely written. They have not yet been copied or distributed.

SUPERBA. Madam Clerk –

PEEL. And can you tell me why you haven't copied them?

SUPERBA. Madam Clerk –

ASSALONE.	**BREEDING**.
Mr. Mayor, I suggest that we move on to –	Peel, this has gone on long enough –

JOHNSON. I haven't copied or distributed them because Mayor Superba asked me not to.

(This hangs in the air.)

OLDFIELD. Friends, we have a serious problem with these ants.

PEEL. *(To* **SUPERBA**.*)* Well, I wonder why that is.

BREEDING. Oh here we go.

PEEL. What do you mean?

BREEDING. I suppose this… so now we've created some vast conspiracy.

PEEL. No, I don't believe that. Why would you say that?

BREEDING. Well. That seems to be what you're insinuating.

PEEL. Frankly, Mr. Breeding, I'm not sure you're bright enough to create a conspiracy.

BREEDING. Excuse me?

PEEL. But you're simple enough to go along with one. Ms. Johnson, will you please read me the minutes from the meeting of October twenty-fifth?

ASSALONE. Point of order.

SUPERBA. You'll need to make a motion to hear those minutes, Mr. Peel.

PEEL. I move that Madam Clerk reads us the minutes from the October twenty-fifth meeting.

(Pause.)

SUPERBA. I'm afraid you need a second, Mr. Peel.

*(**PEEL** stares at **BLAKE**.)*

Anyone? Second?

(No response.)

In absence of a second –

HANRATTY. Second. I second the motion.

SUPERBA. Very well. Motion on the floor that Ms. Johnson reads us the minutes from the meeting on October twenty-fifth.

JOHNSON. Mr. Assalone.

ASSALONE. Assalone, no.

JOHNSON. Mr. Blake.

(Pause.)

BLAKE. Yes.

JOHNSON. Mr. Breeding.

BREEDING. No.

JOHNSON. Mr. Hanratty.

HANRATTY. Yes.

JOHNSON. Ms. Innes.

INNES. No.

JOHNSON. Ms. Matz.

MATZ. Yes. I mean no.

JOHNSON. Mr. Oldfield.

OLDFIELD. *(Glaring at* **ASSALONE.***)* Yes.

JOHNSON. Mr. Peel.

PEEL. Yes.

JOHNSON. Mayor Superba.

(Silence.)

Mayor Superba. Four votes no, and four votes yes.

SUPERBA. Yes, by all means, read the minutes.

JOHNSON. The motion carries.

SUPERBA. Read on, Ms. Johnson.

*(**JOHNSON** stands. Everyone else settles in for the reading.)*

JOHNSON. "Big Cherry City Council Meeting. Tuesday, October twenty-fifth. Minutes."

(She clears her throat.)

"Attendance: V. Assalone, R. Blake, M. Breeding, J. Carp, H. Hanratty, G. Innes, B. Matz, G. Oldfield, Mayor Superba. Staff: D. Johnson, Clerk. Not in attendance: B. Peel. Guests: None, closed session."

(She clears her throat again, takes a drink of water.)

JOHNSON. "Number One. Welcome and Overview. Mayor Superba called the meeting to order at 7:01 p.m. and, due to the closed meeting, dispensed with the invocation. The council recited the Pledge of Allegiance. Mayor Superba then asked if there were any announcements. Mr. Carp then announced to the group that Mr. Peel was not in attendance because his mother had just passed away and Mr. Peel was attending her funeral on the coast. Mr. Carp then passed around a sympathy card for Mr. Peel and all the members of the board signed it. Mr. Carp planned to present the card to Mr. Peel at the next board meeting."

*(Pause. **BREEDING** glances at Carp's empty station, picks up a card in a sealed envelope, and passes it down the line of **MEMBERS** until it reaches **PEEL**.)*

"Number Two. The minutes of the meeting of October eighteenth were submitted and approved. (APP-X 972, 'COBC Co. Meeting Min.,' 10/25.)"

(A few side-eyed glances.)

"Number Three. Mayor Superba began the meeting with an acknowledgment of the success of the Big Cherry Savages, undefeated so far this year. Two of the team's players, Kyle Murray and Danny Coldiron, had been named co-recipients of Defensive Player of the Month in the 4-A Division. The council discussed creating a proclamation for the Savages and designating a specific date as 'Big Cherry Savages Day,' but decided to wait and see how they fared in the playoffs. This decision has been postponed as an agenda item until January of the new year."

(Pause.)

"Number Four. Mayor Superba then, by proclamation, declared November as Eye Injury Prevention Month in Big Cherry. The proclamation was intended to be presented to Dr. Mahendra Puri but he was unable to attend the meeting. The City delivered the proclamation to his offices at the Big Cherry Eye Institute. (APP-X 973, 'Eye Inj. Prev. Mo.,' 10/25.)"

(Pause.)

"Number Five. The council then turned to the subject of the upcoming Big Cherry Heritage Festival. There was a lot of discussion about the importance of this year's festival in particular, for two reasons: First, November 29 will be the sesquicentennial of the Battle at Mackie Creek, and second, attendance has been steadily dropping at the festival for twelve consecutive years and the festival now consistently operates at a deficit. In the interest of generating greater income for the festival, Mr. Blake proposed an attraction called 'Lincoln Smackdown.' Some discussion about the attraction followed and Mr. Blake agreed to develop the idea further before reintroducing it to the group."

(Pause.)

"Mr. Carp continued discussion of the Festival, raising the issue of lost and stolen bicycles, held in a City of Big Cherry warehouse. After some investigation, Mr. Carp had discovered that Sheriff Assalone was selling these items on eBay and using the proceeds to rent a privately-owned fire engine from his brother, Councilman Assalone, which is used for entertainment purposes in the Big Cherry Heritage Festival. Mr. Breeding pointed out the fire engine has become one of the trademarks of the festival, and its image has been used in the festival's publicity materials for a number of years. Mr. Carp countered that the sheriff was handing city funds over to his brother, that the rent for the fire engine was astronomical, and that the bicycles would serve a greater good in the community if they were given to low-income children rather than to the festival. Mr. Carp went on to say that he had taken a low view of the festival and suggested that the community might be better off without it. This view was rejected and Mr. Carp's tenure with the council was completed. (NB: APP-X 974, 'Tr. Carp on BCHF,' 10/25.)"

(Pause. **JOHNSON** *drinks water.)*

"Given the high emotion of the proceedings, Mayor Superba called an end to the meeting before any other agenda items could be considered. Closing ceremony. The meeting concluded at 8:18 p.m."

*(***JOHNSON*** *looks up from the minutes at* ***PEEL***.)*

"Minutes comp., DJ, 10/26."

(A moment.)

SUPERBA. *(To* **PEEL***.)* I hope that answers your questions.

ASSALONE. Yeah, I don't know, maybe she should read it again and I could live through it a *third time.*

PEEL. May I see that, please?

*(***JOHNSON*** *looks to* ***SUPERBA***, *who shrugs. She hands the minutes to* ***PEEL***.)*

ASSALONE. I don't appreciate the suggestion that we aren't doing our jobs well. This council's been around a long time, y'know, and it was doing just fine even before you showed up.

SUPERBA. Mr. Assalone –

ASSALONE. I'm sure you're very eager to make your contribution but trust me, Big Cherry runs like a top.

*(Lights flicker, buzz back on. Again, **PEEL** seems to be the only one who notices.)*

SUPERBA. It's all right. Mr. Peel is new to our council and so deserves every benefit of the doubt.

BREEDING. Hear, hear.

SUPERBA. We are still on Agenda Item 7.2, Mr. Blake's proposal for an attraction called Lincoln Smackdown. Mr. Blake, further discussion?

BLAKE. Mr. Mayor, I'd like to draw up two proposals, one for the temporary version of the attraction, to be used only during the Big Cherry Heritage Festival, and the other to be a permanent attraction, housed in its own purpose-built steel cage, somewhere in the vicinity of –

PEEL. "NB"?

BLAKE. Sorry?

PEEL. *(To **JOHNSON**.)* "NB"?

(A hesitation.)

(Pointing at the page.) "NB"?

SUPERBA. Yes, Mr. Peel?

PEEL. I see the notation "NB" at the conclusion of Number Five, the paragraph concerning Mr. Carp's interaction with the council.

(Silence.)

(Reads.) "...View was rejected and Mr. Carp's tenure with the council was completed. (*NB*: APP-X 974, 'Tr. Carp on BCHF,' 10/25.)"

SUPERBA. A secretarial notation.

BREEDING. Boilerplate.

ASSALONE. So now we're going to examine the footnotes?

PEEL. I know what "NB" means.

ASSALONE. Maybe you could do an in-depth study of the page numbers.

PEEL. "Nota bene."

ASSALONE. Maybe you're going to expose the conspiracy of the *font*.

PEEL. "Nota bene." Anyone?

ASSALONE. How much more of this are we going to put up with?

MATZ. The world is coming down on top of me.

PEEL. Ms. Johnson? "Nota bene"?

ASSALONE. Mr. Mayor?

JOHNSON. "Note well."

PEEL. "Note well."

(*To the group.*) It's Latin. I know a little Latin. Because *I*…am a dentist. And "nota bene" means "note well." You write "NB," followed by a colon, followed by "APP-X 974, 'Tr. Carp on BCHF.'" "APP-X" is appendix?

JOHNSON. Yes.

PEEL. "974" is the number label of the appendix?

JOHNSON. Yes.

PEEL. And "Tr." is…

PEEL.	**JOHNSON.**
Transcript.	Transcript.

SUPERBA. Transcript?

PEEL. Transcript.

SUPERBA. (*To* **JOHNSON.**) Transcript?

JOHNSON. Transcript.

PEEL. "'Note well' the transcript of Mr. Carp's discussion with the board."

SUPERBA. *(Still to* **JOHNSON**.*)* Why would you make a transcript?

JOHNSON. I'm good at my job.

PEEL. I'd like to hear the transcript of "Carp on BCHF."

SUPERBA. You'll need to make a motion to hear –

PEEL. No, I don't. That transcript is noted as an appendix to these minutes. We've already voted to read these minutes. And now I want to hear that transcript.

MATZ. I'm on a lot of medication.

ASSALONE. Mr. Mayor, I'm not going to sit here and –

PEEL. You *are* going to sit there, Mr. Assalone –!

> (**SUPERBA** *pounds the gavel.*)

– you *are* going to sit there and…"nota bene."

> *(Lightning strikes. Lights flicker and shift.* **MR. CARP** *now sits with the council. It is one week earlier.* **SUPERBA** *raps his gavel.)*

BREEDING.	**CARP**.
That fire engine has become one of the trademarks of the festival –!	The sheriff is handing city funds over to his brother!
	ASSALONE.
– It's been used as publicity for as long as I can remember!	He's not *handing* me anything, I own the goddamn fire engine, I'm providing the city with a *service* –!

CARP. The rent you charge is astronomical!

ASSALONE. That's my business! It's still a free market –!

SUPERBA.   Gentlemen, please, let's have a respectful discourse, Mr. Carp has the floor.

CARP. Mr. Mayor, setting aside for the moment the brazen graft, which may be criminally actionable, those bikes would serve a greater good in our community if they were given to low-income children rather than to the festival.

INNES. Mr. Mayor, if I may?

SUPERBA. Yes, Ms. Innes.

INNES. I think everyone here knows how much I adore low-income children. But this seems to me a question of priorities. Is it possible Mr. Carp simply does not hold our Heritage Festival in high esteem?

(The members note **CARP***'s discomfort.)*

SUPERBA. It's a fair question, Mr. Carp.

CARP. No. I do not hold our Heritage Festival in high esteem.

(Outrage! Heresy!)

Whoa, whoa, whoa, hold your horses! Give me a minute! Please!

(Collects his thoughts.)

George, do you remember where you first heard the story of the Battle at Mackie Creek?

OLDFIELD. Church, I think. Or school. I can't tell the difference.

CARP. Ms. Innes?

INNES. Church, I imagine.

CARP. Me too. When I was a boy growing up in Big Cherry. I used to hear that story in Sunday School. And you all remember we used to re-enact the battle, perform it, get in our little costumes and act out all the parts at the Heritage Festival. "Here is your future." Well, God help me, I got curious. And I got it in my head to go looking for that story. I looked online and I found a couple of little things here and there, but I couldn't find anything specific about Otto Pym, so I wrote a couple of emails. I wrote one to Deborah Farmer's great-grandkids but I never heard back. I'm not surprised, they're all oil bigwigs now, no time for a little town like Big Cherry. So I wrote an email to the U.S. Army and I'll be darned if a month later they didn't write me back. Said yes, they had a record of Otto Pym, and in fact, he had been given the Medal of Honor. And I thought, well, there's all the proof of the story anyone would ever need, and it made me proud, like I was still that little boy thrilling to the adventures of Sergeant Otto Pym. But then one other thing they wrote caught my eye, it said that Otto Pym was one of twenty soldiers to receive commendations for their part in the Battle at Mackie Creek. And I thought *"Twenty?"* That doesn't jibe with the story of eight horse soldiers I'd heard all my life. That got me thinking I should dig into it a little further. And I had a devil of a time finding anything else about it, and I tried looking into old newspapers and old textbooks. I wrote historical societies and Old West magazines and book authors, everyone I could think of. And finally my daughter-in-law said, "Have you tried talking to any Native Americans?" I pretty much laughed in her face. But then I got terrifically embarrassed. It was so obvious. And it truly had never occurred to me. Well...turns out the library at the junior college over in Grassland has an archive of local Native history. So I went over there and poked 'round a few Sundays and then one day, I came upon this file, handwritten and mimeographed, bound up with rubber bands and shoved in the bottom of a file cabinet, a bunch of oral histories, and one in particular, with your indulgence, I'd like to read some of it to you. I hadn't planned to get into all this with you tonight, I really didn't. I'm sorry I have to get into this at all. But some things need doing. And here we are. So strap in. This is an oral history, transcribed in 1942... by a schoolgirl at the Mackie Creek Indian Agricultural Academy, a boarding school now long gone, used to be on the farm-to-market road out by the water-treatment plant. The girl who took down this history is named Shannon Red Star, and she is transcribing a story told to her by her grandmother, a woman who was at the Battle at Mackie Creek. And her name was Makawee...

(**CARP** *puts on reading glasses.*)

"A boy from our camp had gone out for days to hunt. He came back very excited. He told the men he had found a big herd one-day's ride away. And a group of the men rode out with that boy to find the four-leggeds. They were excited because the herds had become so sparse and the freezing moon was coming. We lived by the river, we were the people who gather fish from the water, but four-legged beings meant we could get through the freezing moon. So they rode away. And it was that night that the soldiers showed up in our camp. It was like they knew the men would be away. And they made us get out and come stand in front of them while they went through our lodges and searched us. They said we had stolen eggs from a white family near to us along the river. I don't know if anyone had stolen eggs but why would we, we had our own chickens and our own eggs. They made all the men show them their guns and put their guns in a pile. But the only men there were the elders who could not hunt. And one of the men was deaf and so he could not hear what the soldiers were yelling at him and he did not know why they were trying to grab his gun. And they wrestled with the gun and it went off and suddenly they were shooting at us. There were so many soldiers and there were not many of us, we were old men and women and children. We ran for the river but they rode after us and they were shooting us. Some women swam into the water away so far to get away from the shooting but the water was so cold and the water took them. I ran down the bank of the river as fast as I could go and I was pulling a girl with me, a little girl who was not mine but she was too young and she could not run as fast as me. I pulled her with me down the riverbank into the dark. I could hear the shooting behind me but I did not turn around, I just ran. The girl could not keep up but I was pulling her down the bank. And then we heard the horse behind us and the girl screamed but the soldier shot her and she went still. I went into the river then and hid in the freezing water. He shot his gun into the water but the water spirit took me and hid me. I saw him get off his horse and take his knife and take the ear from the girl who ran with me. And he put the ear on a string with other ears and he wore that string around his neck. They killed one hundred and twenty-two of us that night, mostly women and children. When the hunters rode back to the camp, the soldiers said they had started the fighting and the soldiers marched them back to the soldiers' fort and put them in the stockade, and they marched us to the reservation. They gave a lot of those soldiers medals for what they had done that night. The first white family who lived where our relatives used to found oil here in this ground and they became very rich from the Earth and started the town here. And do you know they named the town after us? Because what those men called us was 'cherry niggers' and that is how this town got its name."

(**CARP** *lowers the paper.* **BLAKE** *takes his seat.*)

Forgive me, Bob.

(*Silence.*)

CARP. Well. Now you know why I no longer hold our Heritage Festival in high esteem. In fact, after I read this, I thought probably our best course of action would be to burn that goddamn Heritage Festival to the ground. But I'm not really the burning kind. And after some reflection, I realized maybe we could *use* that festival. In a *new* way. To teach people around here some of our *actual* heritage. I don't know anyone who wouldn't benefit from some unvarnished truth. Folks? We have to tell this story. We have to reconcile this. Make reparations, where possible.

ASSALONE. "Reparations."

CARP. How about apologize, that would be a good start.

BREEDING. What do *we* have to apologize for?

CARP. For all of it, Matt. We have to apologize for all of it.

BREEDING. I haven't done anything.

CARP. Yes, you have too, every time you repeat that fairy tale about Sergeant Otto Pym. I've done it too. We all have. This document isn't just a repudiation, it's an opportunity, and this council could take the wheel on this issue. In one stroke we could begin to manage our guilt and start to make room for everyone in this town. You know, this community is not solely comprised of the descendants of German and Irish settlers or of Mr. Blake's ancestors but also of the people who survived this massacre.

BREEDING. You believe that? That the descendants of this tribe still live in this town?

CARP. No, we killed most of them. But Ms. Red Star, who wrote this down for her grandmother, and who is now a very old lady herself, lives in a nursing home with *your* mother, Matt.

HANRATTY. Mr. Carp, I agree with you, it is a remarkable document and I do believe it deserves a public airing... provided we're able to corroborate this woman's story. I think the more prudent way forward would be for us to table this until after this year's Heritage Festival.

INNES & BREEDING. Hear hear.

HANRATTY. Let's agree to keep this under wraps until then, and then we can create a committee, a research committee, devoted to digging into this topic –

CARP. This woman's story has found its way to me after a hundred and fifty years and I'll be goddamned if I'm just going to send it off to die in some committee. Look, I know we can all get stuck in our ways around here, but this is the true story of our town. I know it and you know it. If this council won't face its responsibility, I'll take this to the newspaper and get this published straight away.

BREEDING. Carp, I play golf every weekend with Jim Rutherford. He's the editor of the *Big Cherry Record* and I doubt he'd be too interested in a story like this.

CARP. Then I'll take it to over to the *Grassland Democrat*, you know they'll publish it. Someone will publish it. I'll get my kids to put it on their computers. Facebook.

SUPERBA. Mr. Carp. The issue before this council concerns the use of funds derived from sales of recovered bicycles. You've traveled somewhat far afield.

CARP. The issue before this council is a lot bigger than bicycles. The issue before this council is just what kind of community do you want to live in. We have built this town on a fiction. And we perpetrate that fiction every day.

OLDFIELD. Well I didn't think I was coming in here tonight to get brow-beaten.

CARP. You deserve a brow-beating, George. There's an old lady who lives in our town whose ancestors were slaughtered so we could build a Rexall Drug. She woke up every day in a town named for a slur on her ethnicity. Why wouldn't we stand up for her?

(**CARP** *takes in the whole assembly.*)

What is a town anyway? You think it's just an imaginary fence built around twenty-five square miles? And the people who live inside it are just random strangers scrabbling for advantage over one another? Isn't the idea of a town bigger than that? Isn't a town the idea itself? That in the place where we send our children to schools together and where we break bread together and where we die together, that we owe each other some simple goddamn decency?

(*No response.*)

ASSALONE. How did you know about those bicycles in the city locker?

CARP. What?

ASSALONE. That warehouse locker where those bikes are stored, that's a secure facility, city property.

CARP. What does that have to do with anything?

ASSALONE. You have access to the city locker?

CARP. No.

ASSALONE. Legal access, I mean?

CARP. No.

ASSALONE. Okay.

CARP. What are you saying, Vince?

ASSALONE. I'm not saying anything.

CARP. It sounds like you're threatening me.

ASSALONE. It does?

BREEDING. I didn't hear anything that even resembled a threat.

ASSALONE. I'm just curious, because that was what we were talking about. The bicycles in the city locker. Someone busted in over there.

CARP. Is that right?

ASSALONE. Someone did.

CARP. You think I did?

ASSALONE. I don't think that. I don't think that. But my brother's on his way here and he has some questions he wants to ask you.

CARP. What're you guys gonna do, make me disappear?

> *(Lights shift back to present-day.* **CARP** *is gone.* **JOHNSON** *lowers the transcript.)*

SUPERBA. Okay, thank you, Ms. Johnson. Now back to the topic at hand. "Lincoln Smackdown." Mr. Blake, I believe you had the floor.

BLAKE. What?

SUPERBA. You have the floor, Mr. Blake. This is your cause. "Lincoln Smackdown."

BLAKE. *(Pause, then: sick.)* I. I need to table this for now. Maybe I can present something new to the group next week.

PEEL. *(To* **SUPERBA.***)* What have you done?

SUPERBA. Moving on to New Business. Item 8.1 concerns a resolution which stipulates "One: That Sergeant Otto Pym's triumph over the Sioux uprising is the Official History of Big Cherry and Two: That Big Cherry Public Schools will advance *only* this official history, enabling a rising generation to better understand the principles of the founding of Big Cherry."

PEEL. What in God's name have you done?

SUPERBA. Mr. Peel, we operate here under Robert's Rules of Order. And I must insist that we adhere to the rules. Or we will have total chaos.

PEEL. Are you insane? Ms. Johnson. Where is Mr. Carp?

(**JOHNSON** *can't look at him.*)

Ms. Johnson!

JOHNSON. I'm a committed public servant.

PEEL. I don't understand, you helped me. You were helping me.

JOHNSON. It wasn't personal. I don't agree with shutting down the discourse. And I think Mr. Carp made some valid points –

PEEL. Because Mr. Carp is an honorable man.

JOHNSON. – But I have a little girl now and I don't have the luxury of these ideas.

(*Beat.*)

We live here. This is where we live.

PEEL. I live here too. And I'm going to find Mr. Carp.

SUPERBA. We all admire your verve, Mr. Peel, but I urge you to calm down and discuss this with the council.

PEEL. Because you're such reasonable people.

SUPERBA. Because this is the forum by which our society rules itself. This is our system and you can either work from inside it or from outside. You'll affect more change from within.

PEEL. *Mr. Carp* tried working from within. And you've silenced him, somehow. Just because you object to your own history.

SUPERBA. History…is a verb.

Your little girl, Justine. You say she's eighteen months?

PEEL. Yes…

SUPERBA. Just starting to walk, developing her vocabulary?

PEEL. Yes…

SUPERBA. I'm curious, are you teaching her the difference between right and wrong?

PEEL. What are you saying to me?

SUPERBA. I doubt you are. You're doing what every new parent does: you're just trying to keep her alive. You're teaching her the animal act of self-preservation. Look around this room: We have children too. We want them to flourish and thrive. We want to give them agency and means and power. And hope. We want them to look forward to the next generation, and the generation after that. Not the generation behind them. What amazing things our children will accomplish.

PEEL. Of course we all want the best for our children, Mr. Mayor, but the *way* you give them that future *matters*. The way you conduct yourself *matters*. The lessons you teach your children, the examples you set for them, who you are…it *matters*.

SUPERBA. "Who you are"? Wait a minute, don't you mean "we"? Aren't *you* one of us?

PEEL. I'm nothing like you.

SUPERBA. Go on, get out of here, go run and get in your SUV – you do have an SUV, yes? You don't like it, it consumes a terrific amount of energy to drive just one family around, and it spews toxic material into our atmosphere, but you got it anyway because it hurts your wife's back to put a baby in the car seat of a sedan – I have an SUV too – get in your SUV and drive through the rain to your two-story house. Kiss your wife and baby and then pour yourself a drink, a single malt, or get a snack, sit down in front of the computer, and start posting some of your outrage on social media. Call a congressman in the morning, after a good night's sleep in your king-sized bed, and be sure to leave him a thoroughly scalding message, demanding justice for Mr. Carp. But sometime tonight, when the temperature of your home drops to a specific mark and you hear the heater come on because that's what you've programmed it to do, remember that you live in a cocoon of comfort and safety because a lot of people who came before you weren't afraid to get their hands dirty.

(**PEEL** *staggers toward the door.* **SUPERBA***'s words stop him:*)

Imagine two futures for your daughter. One in which she is Debbie Farmer, held tight in the bosom of her family, and the world before her is open and fertile; and the other in which she is the little Indian girl running down that riverbank, her last moments lived in blind terror.

(**PEEL** *exits, frightened.*)

(*One by one, the* **MEMBERS** *rise from their seats and move to* **SUPERBA**, *affirming their commitment. Once they've all gathered, he leads them in rhythmic movement. They pound on their chests and stomp their feet. The movement grows in intensity, becoming personalized for each* **MEMBER** *as it grows – some* **MEMBERS** *fall to their knees, some thrash wildly, approaching ecstasy.*)

(**PEEL** *re-enters, soaked. He is destroyed.*)

(*The* **MEMBERS** *embrace him.*)

INNES. Welcome back, Mr. Peel.